Saturn Rising Enterprise

SPIRITUAL UNIVERSAL CHRONICLE MEDIA

T. L. NETHERLY AA. BS. MA.
HUMAN BEHAVIOR
AKA
Ancient Saturn Being City Cat

Printed in the United States of America

ISBN: 9798846577909

10 9 8 7 6 5 4 3 2 1

EMPIRE PUBLISHING
www.empirebookpublishing.com

Saturn Rising Enterprise: Spiritual Universal Chronicle Media dysfunction of Human Behavior where spiritual narc survivors, divine beings are having human experiences living in costumes pretending to be human while wearing the mask of many faces. Allegedly, Narcissistic demonic beings have entered the physical realm illegally to kill, steal, and destroy narc survivors, divine beings. Allegedly, many will deny or disclaim this truth the truth is visible for all to see. Nothing is hidden in the spirit world. I create and write to protect narc survivors based upon my own personal experiences as a narc survivor. Unfortunately, I was neither prepared, warned to comprehend nor understand who or what I was entertaining upon my arrival of planet earth. Narcissistic demonic beings are among the physical realm wearing costumes of destruction pretending to be human while falsely wearing deceptive mask of family, friends, educators, associates, doctors, political, government officials, the elite, etc. Due to the hype, presentations of illusions, the ancient plastic surgery masters of ancient slices of illusions entered the physical realm for the role of a lifetime reconstructing, redesigning what God has created. Remember, everybody wants to be a star in the eyesight of God. This is live entertainment for the heavens. Welcome to Gods Theatre. Where nothing is hidden in the eyesight of the Gods and the heavens. Nothing goes unheard or unseen in the spiritual realm. Nothing is forgotten or unnoticed as a NDB's illusion of self is altered for the costume of a lifetime. Slit, snatch, stitch, seal and go. Chaos and confusion are among the land of go monster go, soul destruction, soul thieves, and soul reconstruction. Wear the costume of your choice for one is having an illegal human experience therefore change in appearances are mandatory for NDB. NDB, are required to wear the mask of human beings to hide, mask who and what they are real life demons playing a wicked game of deception their veil of secrecy has been exposed for all divine beings to witness. Allegedly, NDB, are being exposed for all to view real life demonic beings performing illegally living in costumes and pretending to be human. NDB, ungodly acts of insincere hate, rage, exposed against a certain class of divine beings daily is unacceptable. NDB's, use of lies, conditioning, black magic, fear, wicked manmade chemicals, isolation, lies, trickery, deceit, manipulation, mass hysteria, cannibalism, child endangerment, false imprisonment, gang stalking, envious jealousy, hood rats, gutter snakes, hood demons, hood monsters, hood threats, hood set ups, hood killings in-order to confuse narc survivors, divine beings from achieving, accomplishing their spiritual missions. Allegedly, Spiritual exposure is mandatory for divine beings who have entered the realm of planet e on the behalf of Gods of the ancients for the betterment of humanity must be protected. The power of sincere true prayer is needed for the downfall, the demise of egotistical unhuman, unloving, insincere NDB's, who enter realms to kill, steal, and destroy divine beings without a sincere righteous cause. The betrayal, deceit, trickery of NDB. I experienced caused me to question the existence of God, ancient ancestors, personal angels, spirit guides, angelic animal kingdom angels, angelic fairies. NDB, ratchet evil behaviors attempted to destroy me, a narc survivor known spiritually as the righteous of the land, earth angel a divine being. My role as a Lion Goddess, writer, author, creator by design is to protect warn narc survivors about the behaviors and plans of destruction caused by the NDB, against divine beings. Allegedly, Planet earth has entered the black hole floating throughout metagalaxies rotating universal pickups and drop offs from distant planets. Divine angelic beings and wicked vile NDB, enter this realm by beings tampering with ancient magic, opening ancient doors that were to remain closed for a reason. I write and create based upon my personal experiences in this lifetime of entertaining narcissistic demonic beings who I was condition to believe only existed in the media. Bullshit. I can and will tell you based upon my experience monsters do exist.

Universal Prayer for Narc Survivors

Dear most-high God above all Gods of the universe. I come to you the only way I know how through the power of prayer asking you to bless the minds of narc survivors who depend on you. Most-high God. We need you to show up show out on the world stage of life on our behalf you know each situation. There is nothing new under the sun. Upon great request narc survivors ask for justice punish narcissistic demonic being great destroyers dream killers who wear the mask of many faces living in costumes pretending to be parents our first teachers in the life school. Narcissistic demonic being perpetrating as parents purposely destroy children, divine beings before divine beings become spiritually aware of who they are spiritually. The degrading low-level wicked behaviors of narcissistic demonic beings posing as parents high profile citizens deliberately destroy divine beings by displaying behaviors of wicked evils. Narcissistic demonic beings are monsters hidden in the closets of real-life fairy tales of hell on earth who purposely enter physical realms to kill, steal and destroy families, people, places and naturally blessed environments. Most-high God. Bless the minds, body and soul of narc survivors for our trials and tribulations endured with narcissistic demonic beings are horrific. Bless our minds. Bless us in abundance with spiritual mental peace. Bless the government to be a blessing not a curse to the people. Give the government the minds to sincerely do right by your people. Put love in their hearts for the hearts of humanity depend on sincere world leaders for basic survival. Destroy narcissistic demonic beings who enter to kill steal destroy us. In the event my prayer is not practical, just expose every crooked narcissistic demonic being in high seats of power. Most-high God. Could you personally escort narcissistic demonic beings back to the pits of hell during such confusing times? Most-high God. Narcissistic demonic beings of power are out of control playing with people lives. The lives of divine beings are not a joke. Narcissistic demonic being manmade laws of dysfunction have expired. Most-high God above all Gods of the universe. You see all the chaos, dysfunction, lies, plot scenes live on the world stage of life please shut down production. Welcome to God's Theatre. Where nothing is hidden in the eyesight of God. Nothing is hidden from you most-high God above all Gods in the universe. My prayers are activated immediately the appointed time has arrived narcissistic demonic beings will be escorted to hell upon the request of divine beings who enter the realm to restore love. Most-high God above all Gods ever planted in the universe. Bless every pastor to speak your words not the words or beliefs of narcissistic demonic beings who live, sit, and roam church houses causing havoc and spiritual destruction among the church members. In closing, Most-high God, I ask that you cover our children your divine beings need immediate spiritual protection from narcissistic demonic being. The evil behaviors of narcissistic demonic beings are seen throughout history nothing is hidden in the spirit world. I claim this prayer in truth in honor of divine beings who enter this realm on behalf of sincere love. I claim this prayer to be the end the demise of narcissistic demonic beings who enter to kill, steal and destroy divine beings. Most-high God. Bless our angelic ancestor angels in abundance with spiritual high honors our angels are sincere angels who go above and beyond the call of duty. Bless my angelic ancestors of the highest spiritual courts who stood guard as black magic failed against me for my demise from low vile wicked immediate family members, associates, hidden haters. Bless my Caucasian, German great grandfather for loving me, protecting, watching over me. Bless, Eayler Clark, for loving me when I was born in families of narcissistic demonic beings who despised me, my presence, upon arrival into the earth realm. I am forever grateful for all of my sacred angels, earth angels in spirit who I adore. Narc survivors, In the name of spiritual truth. I send love, peace, abundance, prosperity to you. The forever beautiful, sexy beings of the metagalaxy of love T. L. Nthrly. AA. BS. MA Human Behavior. The creator, writer, producer of Saturn Rising Enterprise universal chronicles

Saturn Rising Enterprise Universal Chronicles: Introduction of Synopsis

Saturn Rising Enterprise literature from Saturn Rising Universal Chronicles Minizine. Saturn Rising, Minizine Magazine is based on creativity, edgy, raw, social, spiritual science fiction stories of Saturnarians. Present-day narc survivors, earth angels, divine beings who have spiritually fought armies of narcissistic demonic beings vicious wicked demonic bullies that enter, dwell on planet earth illegally to kill, steal and destroy divine beings without a sincere righteous cause.

Allegedly, My Darling, narc survivor, reader, observer watchers of a blessed unique universe. I write out of sincere concern based upon my life experiences; lessons learned during my personal human experience while dwelling on planet E. However, I have aged gracefully, due to trauma I endured along the way with the help of sincere true loving adoring angels who caught me each time I was knocked down. I am forever grateful for the blessing honor of angels who watch over me during my spiritual journey. It has taken me five thousand four hundred years to reach my destination with this important information. I am ancient Santurnarian. I, have traveled lifetimes to reach you. My Darling, Narc survivor my spirit unchained broken free my soul awoken from a dreadful slumber of black magic, trickery, fuckery of ancient NDB's used to bind me forever so that I, I would never be able to reveal the existence of narcissistic demonic beings exist on planet earth walk among divine beings in costumes and mask pretending to be human for the destruction of love, the destruction of humanity.

Allegedly, Ancient vile low level NDB, have been tracking me down since the beginning on time (BCE), before Christ existed. I know. I know, this shit is crazy it does not make since. This is utterly insane to viciously attack divine beings without a sincere righteous cause. NDB, believe they would stop me from delivering such vital information to you, divine beings who enter this realm for the betterment of humanity only to be confused, used, abused and lied to by an outdated belief system that teaches history of hate, history without truth is the historical education of NDB. NDB, tactics to demise and destroy its victims are insane. What I know to be spiritually correct is history without spiritual truth is a damn lie. Be very careful for nothing goes unseen in the eyesight of God. Beware. NDB's, Nothing, is hidden in the eyesight of God. Nothing! Allegedly, I dwell in The City of Lost Angels where you have more NDB, than angels. It is no secret Saturn rising enterprise, high ranking honorable angels from the spiritual world for example shape shifters who wear mask pretending to be human have entered earth realm for the betterment of humanity for divine beings are being destroyed, killed without a sincere righteous cause by NDB, who have entered planet earth illegally to kill, steal and destroy the righteous of the land, earth angels, divine beings before living out their spiritual destiny on planet earth.

The divine beings God invited not that of man but who God invited with high honors to have and enjoy the human experience, so that more angels would be encourage to visit planet earth for the betterment of humanity and love. Allegedly, My Darling Saturnarians, those of you who are living among planet earth know this to be true. Allegedly, this science fiction literature is created for entertainment purposes only. Spiritually speaking, beings entertained or intrigued by the literature of Saturn Rising Enterprise, you, yourself are most likely Saturnarian, or celestial being having a spiritual human experience on planet E. Official Saturnarian greetings to you. Swoopzx. Saturn Rising Enterprise.

Sincerely, Lieutenant Colonel; Goddess Counsel, Narc Survivor, 11th dynasty (BCE) Siobrija Soran, Saturnarian, from Saturn Rising Enterprise.

Silver Queen Mothership of Love

The minizine of an accepting reality, Allegedly, many beings are unaware, clueless to the facts NDB's are allegedly having illegal human experiences in the physical realm.

Welcome to Gods Theatre. Welcome to Saturn Rising Universal Chronicles. Where we Saturnarians, believe in the power of God, at all times know matter what adversity enters our invisible shield of spirit. Greetings all Saturnarians. The ancients of the universe are among us. Peace and blessings upon your entrance into this physical realm of planet E. Narc survivors, angelic beings, divine beings, space children, my autism is beautiful, universal lovers, night birds, majestic shapeshifters, angelic Fairies, angelic animal kingdom angels of high honors, angelic nature orphans. Divine beings who wear the mask of the righteous in the land. We Saturnarians, admire your bold style, courage, defending standing on the front lines for divine beings with a sincere righteous cause forever blessed you are. Saturnarians, of the highest spiritual courts abundantly sincerely bless you with spiritual abundance for you have did an outstanding job in strength and numbers. Divine beings enter the physical realm to face the adversity of NDB, who enter the physical realm illegally without a sincere righteous cause. NDB, enter the physical realm to kill, steal and destroy divine beings. No matter what anybody ever tells you, God is real. The greatest lie ever created, told by NDB, having illegal human experience who enter the physical realm to kill, steal, and destroy the righteous of the land, is that God does not exist. History without the truth is a spiritual lie. Nothing is hidden in the eyesight of God. Nothing. The black book. The Holy Bible states, God has chosen the foolish things of the world to put to shame the wise and God has chosen the weak things of the world to put to shame the things which are mighty and the base things of the world and the things which are despised. God has chosen and the things which are not to bring to nothing the things that are. Being defamed, we entreat. We have been made as the filth of the world, the offscouring of all things until now. I do not write these things to shame you, but as my beloved children I warn you. For we do wrestle against flesh and blood against principalities, against powers, against the rulers of darkness of this age, against spiritual host of wickedness in the heavenly places. We speak the wisdom of God in a mystery, the hidden wisdom which God ordained before the ages for our glory. Which none of the rulers of this age knew, for had they known, they would not have crucified the Lord of glory. Do not forget to entertain strangers for by so doing some have unwittingly entertained angels. In the wisdom of God, the world through wisdom did not know God. It, pleased God through the message preached to save those who believe. Praying always with all prayer and supplication in the spirit, being watchful to this end with all perseverance. For we do not wrestle against flesh and blood but against principalities, against powers, against the rulers of the darkness of this age, against spiritual host of wickedness in the heavenly places. God has chosen the foolish things of the world to put to shame the wise, and God has chosen the weak things of the world to put to shame the things which are mighty, the base things of the world and the things which are despised God has chosen, the things which are not, to bring to nothing the things that are. I do not write these things to shame you, but as my beloved children I sincerely warn you.

Saturn Rising Enterprise, Chief Lion Goddess Protector: Daughter of The Rising Sun Spiritual Council, City Cat, Puss in Boots, Gun-in garter belt loaded at all times. Swoop. Swoop. Swoop. Bang, Bang, Bang

Foundation of the righteous headquarters to spiritually protect and serve the righteous of the physical realm

How to successfully avoid, conquer, recognize Narcissistic Demonic Beings - deceitful energy of wicked behaviors within your human experience:

Created & Written by the infamous, narc survivor Agent 357 (B.C.E) Lionesses Goddess Federation of righteousness spiritual ancient wisdom the creator of a social society. This is a journey of my personal experiences in this lifetime. God is real. No, matter what any being tells you. God is real. Ancients are immortal spiritual divine beings hidden spiritual spies who keep record of everything, every microscopic morsel of the life experience is spiritually recorded. There are no secrets in the spiritual realm, nothing is hidden. This minizine is based on my personal life experiences with NDB's, I entertained without being aware of what and who I was spiritually entertaining or dealing with. The NDB's, in my personal human experience wanted me physically spiritually dead without a sincere righteous cause, upon my arrival, entrance into planet E, evil knows Gods most favored in the universe. The spiritual lifestyle of famous spiritual divine beings having a human experience completing divine missions. Welcome to God's Theatre. Where everybody wants to be a star in the eyesight of God. Unfortunately, the invisible veil has been lifted. I am a majestic shape shifter. I have lived several lifetimes. Queen Feather Mama. I am a proud night bird that flies by the light of the moon. By design I was created to live among planet E. I am the infamous City Cat of the Lion Goddess Federation, sexy by design. God made no mistakes concerning my design. This is for every NDB, that used black magic against me without a sincere righteous cause for my demise. Smile for the camera. I have been shockingly informed of who and what you are. Nothing is hidden in the eyesight of God. This is spiritual entertainment at its best for the heavens. NDB's, that imitate my style, smile in my face throw daggers of hate behind my back smile for the camera wicked by design you are. NDB, rewarded me evil for my good in the eyesight of God. I am pure sincere light. How dare you! You narcissistic demonic beings! Insult my spiritual intelligence. How dare you come for me! I was sincerely invited by the most-high God above all Gods of the universe to enter this realm be who what the hell I choose during my life experience. However, NDB, your false created image, ignorance concerning me is beneath me. I am Spiritual Royalty all that you did to damage, destroy me, I sincerely send back triple fold with blessings. Bow down you ole ancient raggedy dusty bitches, witches, warlocks, flies, monsters, vile sneaky wicked snakes smiling in my face with a deceitful wicked grin! Saturn Rising Enterprise has landed. I arrived prepared for battle. I represent for all divine beings in this lifetime I still look fabulously good. This is for NDB, who happily rewarded me evil for my good. How dare you! You evil wicked energy vampires. How dare you! You wicked narcissistic demonic being's destroyers of divine beings. NDB, Darling. Please, smile for the camera. Darling. Your mask has been revealed. I am exposing evil, wicked behaviors. NDB's, display teeth of the ungodly with upside-down crooked smiles. NDB, how dare you insult my spiritual intelligence. How dare you disturb my spirit! Spiritual Royalty! May God show no mercy on your bitter ratchet rotten soul, deceitful actions towards me. I see the monster behind masks ugly demonic monster by design. Smile, for the camera ignorant monsters. Nothing is hidden in the eyesight of God. This is live spiritual entertainment for the physical realm. Nothing is hidden silly monsters. I survived NDB's, wicked plots to destroy me and so can you. Life experiences are my best experiences. Like Jill Scott said on 826. Huh. What? Narcissistic demonic beings! "You broke me, but I'm healing, You, broke me, but I'm healing". I am spiritual royalty. You messed with the wrong divine being. I expose behaviors of narcissistic demonic beings. Divine crew members fasten your seatbelts lets glide. This spiritual universal ride is known for turbulence, profanity & sexual content. Dress to impress. Narc survivors undercover divine beings restoring love are among you.

General, Sazzie'Sazule

Welcome to Saturn Rising Enterprise. I am General Sazzie'Sazule of Saturn Rising Enterprise. I have entered your realm on behalf of God, for the betterment of humanity throughout metagalaxies. I enter on behalf of divine beings having a human experience. I am an ancient of Saturn Rising Enterprise. I am Santurnarian. Please, relax and enjoy the ride. I ask that you fasten your safety belts prepare for takeoff. I entered your realm to inform divine beings of all ages all children of light, electric beings, space children, universal lovers, majestic shape shifters, narc survivors, my autism is beautiful earth angels, night birds, angelic fairies, animal kingdom angels who wear the mask of fur people, invisible, nonverbal beings, sincere true watchers of the universe for love on behalf of God and mighty archangels of love. I, General, Sazzie'Sazule, entered this realm to inform divine beings who enter this realm on behalf of God. That, the spiritual war is in effect. NDB's, are among planet E. We do not wrestle against flesh and blood, but against principalities against powers against the rulers of the darkness of this age against spiritual host of wickedness in the heavenly places. Therefore, take up the whole amore of God that you may be able to withstand in the evil day having done all to stand above all taking the shield of faith with which you will be able to quench all the fiery darts of the wicked one praying always with all prayer and the supplications in the spirit being watchful.

Do not forget to entertain strangers for by so doing some have unwittingly entertained spiritual angelic beings, giants, generals of spiritual commanders, goddesses, judges of the highest spiritual courts, of the most-high God without being aware of their spiritual presence. Beware many beings have did poorly during earthly test entertaining divine beings who you entertained without being aware spiritually of who or what being you were spiritually entertaining. MMM. Many of you have downright disrespected high archangels living on planet earth in costumes pretending to be human. That is so sad, most of all pathetic in the eyesight of God. This is God's theatre nothing goes unseen. We are all actors beneath the heavens. Everybody wants to be a star in the eyesight of the Gods. Divine beings, vacationing on planet earth living in costumes wearing mask pretending to be human is spiritual entertainment for the heavens. The adventures of traveling through the black hole unprepared.

As it is written, God has chosen the foolish things of the world to put to shame the wise and God has chosen the weak things of the world to put to shame the things which are mighty and the base things of the world and the things which are despised God has chosen and the things which are not to bring to nothing the things that are.

Allegedly, it is said that, I, General, Sazzie'Sazule, of Saturn Rising Enterprise has taken on the mission to defeat, fight NDB, for the sincere cause of love on behalf of love for narc survivors, divine beings that have entered the earths realm on behalf of love. This is my confirmation. I, General, Sazzie'Sazule, of Saturn Rising Enterprise enter this realm on behalf of love, for, I am in love with love for the betterment of all humanity. With gun and sword in hand. I. General, Sazzie'Sazule, enter prepared to slay wicked NDB's, who have infected planet earth with hate, filth and slander. This is personal. Many archangels have fallen at the hands of NDB's. No more! It is over! I declare war immediately against NDB's!

I, General, Sazzie'Sazule, of Saturn Rising Enterprise, gladly accept the invitation. I entered the physical realm to protect divine beings from unrighteousness without a sincere righteous cause to slay NDB, who enter planet E, to kill, steal and destroy divine beings who enter the physical realm on the behalf of love, for love. I, General, Sazzie'Sazule, enter to restore love on behalf of love for the nation of narc survivors

Saturn Rising Enterprise Universal Chronicles Narc Survivors Rescue Elite Mission

Commander in Chief, Sarbaria Saso, Brown Sugar Black Cat Federation 8th Dynasty (BCE)

It is my duty as a spiritual ancient General of divine beings to come forth in all my sexiness in silence to strike on behalf of narc survivors the righteous of the land. Sh. Sh. Sh. Love wants to dance. I shall except this dance my love for peace upon planet earth for, I, am Commander in Chief, Sarbaria Saso. Black Cat Federation 8th Dynasty (BCE). Sexy by design. I enter with an abundance of love that will kill, steal and destroy NDB, who enter planet E, to destroy love for the sake of love. I, Commander in Chief, Sarbaria Saso. Has spoken it shall be done. NDB, must return back to hell immediately. I am the Chronicles of love. I refuse to have waste management of NDB, ruin my party. I laugh in the face of NDB, who enter planet earth illegally for the destruction of love. Love will no longer be defeated by evil. How dare NDB, enter planet E, illegally to kill, steal and destroy innocent divine beings of love without a sincere righteous cause! How dare NDB, go against that which is good for the betterment of humanity! How dare NDB, go against the will of God! How dare NDB! Interrupt my peace on Saturn Rising Enterprise, that I have too personally intervene how dare you inconsiderate, NDB's interrupt love. To interrupt love is the greatest sin of all. How dare you!

However, as always. I, Commander in Chief, Sarbaria Saso. Have entered to slay NDB's, back to the pits of present-day hell, from which NDB's, have escaped for the chance of a lifetime the illegal human experience everybody wants to be a star in the eyesight of God. It's spiritual to perform their interpretation of the human experience for God's Theatre

In the wisdom of God, the world through wisdom did not know God. It, pleased God through the foolishness of the message preached to save those who believe. Do you believe in the power of the most-high God?

Protect your spiritual body cover yourself with personal prayers psalms for example chant a psalm a day before you go out to handle business this will keep NDB, away from your precious energy. Psalm 91, excellent psalm protectors to repel NDB, negative energy. Spiritual truth of ancient wisdom. Ancient Sybil in disguise. Mama Browns favorite, psalm 100. "No matter what anybody ever tells you. God is Real". No matter what a NDB, tells you, God is real, angelic ancestors ancient angels are real. The spirit world is real. NDB, are real demonic beings having illegal human experiences within physical realms near you.

Toot. Toot. Hey. Sleep. Sleep. Wake up divine beings many of you are asleep. Dear children of Saturn Rising, Wake Up! The greatest lie ever told by NDB's, is that God does not exist. The most- high of the universe does exist. I am blessed to know hidden secrets of this blessed universe. For I am spiritual royalty. I am the spiritual orphan of nature upon arrival. I am Spiritual Royalty. I am the rare being who has been spiritually blessed by a host of caring nurturing universal angelic beings that have loved me without a sincere righteous cause. Mother nature adores me. Universal angels protect me. I am a tree planted by the most-high of the universe I shall not be moved by NDB, the known pestilence of planet E. I am forever spiritually grateful for the love of a blessed universe. I have sincere true angels, archangels, spirit guides, animal kingdom angels that love me unconditionally. I have angelic fairies that love me beyond this realm. I have spiritual elementals that treat me like spiritual royalty. I have a spiritual family that loves me un-conditionally. NDB, are not allowed near my energy field. Sh. Sh. Sh. I am ancient warrior sent to kill, steal and destroy NDB's, who disturb narc survivors, the righteous of the land, divine beings, earth angels, my autism is beautiful angelic beings, my disability is divine I'm so damn fine angelic beings, animal kingdom angelic beings, nonverbal angelic beings are prepared for battle. Beware NDB's, your reign is over. Please, NDB, your season has expired

Divine beings enter on behalf of God out of sincere love of humanity to assist, help and repair, rescue a universe in despair due to the illegal entrance of ancient and new NDB, on a planned mission of destruction. NDB, are having illegal human experiences all over the physical realm. NDB, wear the costume mask of many faces while living in costumes pretending to be normal human beings living life purposely causing chaos and havoc within the physical realm. Please do not pretend that you did not see nor witness the behavior of NDB's, near you or feel the behavior of low down, dirty dysfunctional disposition of stank in the atmosphere. Hell. Many knew about lies, scandals, deception, black magic used to cause death and destruction against divine beings who know the spiritual rules and regulations of the human experience. The divine beings who live and let live according to true spiritual laws of the heavens the universe are forever spiritually protected regardless to the belief of NDB. Modern day universal dysfunctional monsters.

Allegedly, due to dysfunction at the junction trying to function in and on a planet engulfed by narcissistic demonic beings who roam the planet freely to destroy all that is good in and for the land of healthy spiritual living. Many visually see, smell the stench of deception the lies and betrayal in the atmosphere but often ignore its presence due to fear of NDB, of power. NDB, ignore, downplay their dysfunctional acts towards the righteous of the land out of spiritual dysfunctional ignorance. Today NDB, will fall be damn back to the pits of hell from which all NDB's have escape. Nothing is hidden from the eyesight of God. Nothing is hidden in the spiritual realm. The physical realm is hurting due to the vicious acts, behaviors of NDB. Mother nature is severely affected by what she spiritually witnesses throughout time by NDB's, in her presence the stealing of land, the illegal poisoning of her God given soil, her children have been negatively affected by inhumane acts of NDB, who enter to kill, steal and destroy divine beings out of envy, jealousy. NDB, pretending to be doctors are promoting medicine of destruction. Lives of NDB's, are spiritually destroyed as divine beings enter realms to protect against the evil abuse caused by NDB's, of life affairs. NDB, who toy with science prepare for a scientific demise. NDB, tampering with the divine soil be prepared for revenge is sweet to the soul of the divine. Mother nature feels in the core of her soul she is alive and aware of every injustice against her set by NDB, of destruction.

As an Ancient Galactic General of Saturn Rising Enterprise, it is my personal duty to inform all divine beings of the physical realm of this unfortunate event in this day and time. Allegedly, Narcissistic demonic beings have entered the physical realm uninvited to kill, steal and destroy divine beings the righteous of the land without a sincere righteous cause. However, Nothing, is hidden in the eyesight of God, and the spiritual realm. Universal divine beings, invisible protectors are fighting spiritual battles. Nothing is hidden. Nothing, especially, the wicked acts of narcissistic demonic beings perform in secret against divine beings as planet E, travels through the black hole. NDB, universal wicked egotistical cowardly acts are obsolete. I stated earlier in this letter, NDB, your time is up on planet earth. Inform all NDB, present within the physical realm your reign is over. Saturn Rising has arrived ready for battle, personally we are not fans of any form of injustice caused by the act of in-humane narcissistic demonic being society. NDB. Who is your leader? Your leader has severely failed its dedicated followers.

Sincerely, Queen Feather Mama: Goddess by design of Spiritual Royalty of ancient Thebes (BCE)

Ancient Galactic General of Saturn Rising: Daughter of the Rising Sun

Welcome Saturn Rising Enterprise

Epigraphs of spiritual conversation in lieu of a preface per introduction of Saturn Rising:

Allegedly, nothing is hidden in the eyesight of God. Nothing is hidden in the spiritual realm. Nothing is hidden in the universe just as nothing is new under the Sun. Narcissistic demonic being behaviors are judged spiritually by those who NDB, choose to destroy. Narcissistic demonic beings have been fooled. Divine beings who narcissistic demonic beings believe did not matter or exist in the eyesight of God are high ranking spiritual commanders, generals and judges in the spiritual realm. Allegedly, Narcissistic demonic beings destroy and entertain ancient divine angels without being aware of their true identity. As ancient Spiritual Royalty. I Walk with Spiritual Giants of a Blessed Universe. Angels are among the living. There are many secrets in the universe show respect for the things that you can, not see the universe might share her secrets with you. If my great ancestors, mother, father tree of roots would speak they would blow your minds with what narcissistic demonic beings believes to be that of a secret, for in a feeble mind no living being saw or witness their dirty deeds plots planted in nature for the destruction of family, love, humanity. There are no hidden secrets in the universe. Nothing is hidden even the trees have eyes the invisible walk, the land freely observing wicked behaviors. There are no secrets in the universe. Nonverbal lies display many truths of hidden truths to distort the truth

History without the truth is a lie. Please be prepared when the universe exposes NDB, dirty big and little secrets throughout his-story of humanity. Hold on to your hats for it is going to be some flip-flopping show-stopping unbelievable events. A sincere universal love of sincere peace is needed to help, heal and repair a broken nation engulf with broken hearts of betrayal, deceit, lies, trickery and the mighty fuckery of all mental illness, the joy of racism caused by NDB, of destruction. Allegedly, Narcissistic demonic beings allegedly condition masses of lost angels to believe in their illusions and lies regarding this lifetime. The manmade distorted history of life is a lie. History without the truth is a lie. Put your trust in God not that of man. In the spirit of the most-high God we trust on Saturn Rising Enterprise. The Chronicles of love, peace not that of war. Narcissistic demonic beings promote universal pauses for destruction of humanity the distorted mask of evil is dissolving quickly. Narcissistic demonic beings promote separation of family for present-day hell, separation of love by make believe laws of NDB, lies and confusion. With sincere love there is no separation of family allowed in nature of any kind, separation of family is not love but that of NDB, control. Smile. For the camera. Silly monsters. I have studied witness deceitful NDB's, behavior towards divine beings without a sincere cause.

Allegedly, a spiritual reality as it was written in the great book of spiritual knowledge. We do not wrestle against flesh and blood, but against principalities against powers against the rulers of darkness of this age. Against spiritual host of wickedness in the heavenly places. Therefore, take up the whole Amor of God that you may be able to withstand in the evil day and having done all to stand above all taking the shield of faith with which you will be able to quench all the fiery darts of the wicked one praying always with all prayers and supplications in the spirit being watchful. However, do not forget to entertain strangers for by so doing, some of you sincerely have unwittingly entertained Angels without being aware of their presence. Allegedly, The, sad reality is that In, the wisdom of God the world through wisdom did not know God. It, pleased God through the foolishness of the message preached to save those who believe. Do you believe in the hidden mysteries of the universe? I do.

Saturn Rising Enterprise Universal Chronicles

Broadcasting commercial interruption service announcement for divine beings.

I am General Sahtibah; National Angel Rescue Champions of Saturn Rising my identification number is narc survivor 222555333 (BCE) I represent the tribe of Judah. The ancient tribe of Saturnarian-lions. I have entered on behalf of God for the betterment of love. I am known for slaying modern day narcissistic demonic beings throughout the history of many lifetimes. Divine beings are forever protected spiritually for nothing is hidden in the eyesight of God. Nothing is hidden. That is why I have traveled so far into your realm my assistance is needed for the exit of all narcissistic demonic beings has arrived. On Saturn Rising Enterprise, we believe in sincere love, peace and harmony throughout the universe there is no room for era when it comes to sincere love. This has been a Saturn Rising Enterprise service announcement. All NDB, exit back to hell from which you have escaped

MUSICAL INTERLUDE

SATURN

By Stevie Wonder & Mike Sembello

Packing my bags going away to a place where the air is clean

On Saturn There's no sense to sit and watch people die

We don't fight our wars the way you do We put back all the things we use

On Saturn There's no sense to keep on doing such crimes

There's no principals in what you say No directions in the things you do

For your world is soon to come to a close Through the ages all great men have taught

Truth and happiness just can't be bought or sold Tell me why you people are so cold

I'm going back to Saturn where the rings all glow Rainbow moonbeams and orange snow

On Saturn People live to be two hundred and five. Going back to Saturn where the people smile

Don't need cars cause we learn to fly On Saturn Just to live to us is just a natural high

We have come here many times before To find your strategy to peace is war

Killing helpless men women and children That don't even know what they are dying for

We can't trust you when you take a stand with gun and bible in your hand

And the cold expression on your face Saying give us what we want or we'll destroy

I'm Going back to Saturn where the rings all glow Rainbow moonbeams orange snow

On Saturn People live to be two hundred and five Going back to Saturn where the people smile

Don't need cars cause we learn to fly On Saturn Just to live to us is our natural high

Saturn Rising Enterprise Universal Chronicles Behavior Files:

The how to guide of noticing and recognizing behavioral traits of NDB often displayed but often ignored.

Allegedly, Narcissistic demonic beings, behavior displays itself without shame or warning unfortunately, if you dwell in the city of Lost Angels or any universal city most likely you have entertained or sat in the midst of a narcissistic demonic being having an illegal human experience. Narcissistic demonic beings cause chaos and havoc in the land NDB's, thrive on the destruction of divine beings. Narcissistic demonic beings love to taunt, torture, and kill in a social society that accepts and promotes the hate, lies and deceit of narcissistic demonic beings, behaviors. Allegedly, Narcissistic demonic beings are sincere bona fide monsters living throughout the universe wearing costumes, mask of human beings. Allegedly, The, earths realm is contaminated with narcissistic demonic beings deceitful degrading behaviors towards divine beings. The, sincere and true divine beings of the universe are narc survivors. Divine beings stand for peace. The righteous and humble of the land are sincerely blessed in the eyesight of God

This literature is for divine beings who live in costumes pretending to be narc survivors. Blessings to beings who stand out boldly in sincere prayer against narcissistic demonic behaviors for a blessed universe in truth and righteousness for the betterment of all of humanity and not just a chosen few. Divine ancient beings are present for the betterment of humanity to restore love. To all prayer warriors blessed sincere and true. The spiritually bold and beautiful. I am referring to all divine beings, earth angels, universal lovers, space children, angel fairies, night birds, fur babies, sugar babies. Greetings. Spirit recognizes spirit. I hear the drums in the distance. I hear the tambourine serenade, step to the side. I have arrived. Gigantic silver bells are ringing for my grand entrance into the earth realm. Hey! Ooh! Greetings! Blessed! Spiritual! I have arrived. Darlings of divine. I am here to teach divine beings and to dispose of NDB. Spiritual school is in session due to the spiritual pause of a discombobulated axle of a contaminated earth due to the wicked distasteful acts of ancient modern day narcissistic demonic beings who have entered the physical realm uninvited to have an illegal human experience wearing the mask of many faces. I have entered from Saturn Rising Enterprise to expose, slay inform NDB, of their demise their time of destruction has been canceled. The scene of NDB, abuse has been written out of the script of the human experience it is over. Love has made a comeback. Love will be taking back the physical realm.

Sincerely, Judge Soca Whales of The Ole' Ancient Animal kingdom in honor of my brothers and sisters who escape the waters of a contaminated ocean caused by noncaring, heartless, non-emotional insensitive narcissistic demonic beings how dare you destroy my family! How dare you destroy my natural God given environment. How dare you destroy me. My waters are contaminated because of ignorance of NDB. NDB, Beware. Spiritually for your ignorance against my waters my family has caused universal hardship for the land and oceans. Narcissistic demonic beings responsible will pay a spiritual price for the disregard, disrespect against mother nature, mother of elements. Nothing is hidden from mighty Gods of the oceans.

Our deepest regards. Saturn Generals ancient sea Goddess, Octopus Queen Red Violet. The ancient Saturn Tortoise God. General of the Black Sea. The infamous stylish Mr. Wiggles. Ritzy Raven, The Blackest Queen Raven of Birdland sponsored by Saturn Owl Café. Saturn's Rising galaxy drifter the infamous City Cat. Ancient elite archangel of the animal kingdom the jet black rare large lion displaying a mane of ancient historical locks of spiritual wisdom of the Cat people of the constellation of Leo

Allegedly, narcissistic demonic behaviors most experienced and known in the universe I have personally experienced.

Allegedly, know, matter what anybody tells you God is real, know, matter how a situation presents itself. God is real. Have a conversation with God about your situation. Pray. Chant a Psalm 91,35,71, 100, Psalms are great spiritual protection. Talk to your Angels and Spirit guides remember there are no hidden secrets in the spirit world, narc survivors." For we do not wrestle against flesh and blood but against principalities, against powers, against the rulers of the darkness of this age, against spiritual host of wickedness in the heavenly places". Narcissistic demonic beings are cowards in the spiritual realm. Fear gives a narcissistic demonic being power over your situation, never surrender your power. Beat NDB, down with the power of prayer. Your words, conversations with God are powerful tools used to defeat NDB, who attack you without warning. Your angels are mighty spiritual giants, warriors, ancient original spiritual gangsters stand before you. You are a divine being the sincere and true divine beings of light. Divine being by design have spiritual intelligence to send narcissistic demonic beings back to the pits of hell from which they escaped. Once the narcissistic demonic being is exposed their hidden costume or mask begin to fade away the monster becomes nonexistent the NDB, can no longer hide in costumes nor pretend to be human a monster has been exposed, revealed for all to witness.

1. Narcissistic demonic beings are unemotional, lack compassion for divine beings and animals. Be bold do

not fear narcissistic demonic beings or their wicked behavior remember you are dealing with a little monster who has escape the pits of hell illegally to cause havoc in your life because you are loved dearly in the eyesight of God. Narcissistic demonic beings do not sincerely believe in God or Angels. Divine beings are invited sincerely on behalf of the most-high God in the universe to have and enjoy the human experience. The NDB, is beneath you envious jealous of you, divine being, narc survivors

2. Narcissistic demonic beings are unemotionally detached from spiritual reality, ignorant in thought. NDB, enter to kill, steal, and destroy divine beings. NDB, have egotistical wicked dispositions. Please believe what you see. Especially when a narcissistic demonic being behavior is noticeable such as innocent killings in public view, lies against the humble of the land, gang stalking, false media tracking, the evil eye, world pauses for destruction, separation of families. Narcissistic demonic beings thrive on chaos and confusion, universal mass hysteria for control.
3. Narcissistic demonic beings are rude, fake, in-sincere individuals. They smile in your face throw daggers behind your back. Smiling faces of narcissistic demonic beings tell lies to protect their deceitful behavior towards divine beings. There are no secrets except monsters, NDB, are having illegal human experiences for the destruction of humanity.
4. Narcissistic demonic beings display wicked dispositions, intentions upon entering this realm with an evil bitter heart. The light in their soul is soul-less, dark with trickery, hate no light exist in their inner core, only

dark matter, jealousy, envy, ancient deceit. Wicked thoughts created plans of destruction to destroy without a sincere cause.

5. Narcissistic demonic beings do not appreciate mother nature. Allow mother nature, the animal kingdom, the elementals to assist you with conquering the wrath of a narcissistic demonic being set in your path to stop your contribution. The universe is alive. Nothing is hidden from mother nature especially the acts of narcissistic demonic beings done in secret.
6. Narcissistic demonic beings are ignorant to spiritual facts there are no known secrets in the spirit world. The invisible world is alive, present. One will be amazed at the things that he or she can-not visually see in the physical realm
7. Narcissistic demonic beings are known as double face, two face wicked evil beings like that of Dr. Jekyll and Mr. Hide, the monster within. Pay attention to the behaviors of a narcissistic demonic beings for they change with the moon watch their behaviors, manners at all times, narcissistic demonic beings cannot hide or suppress who or what they are for too long, eventually the hidden monster inside will revel itself to you. Caution. It is very frightening when a monster reveals itself without warning. Immediately leave that situation behind seek your happiness. Pray NDB, out of your life vacate the premises immediately. Never entertain a narcissistic demonic being when realizing who and what you are dealing with. Beware, leave it alone the monster is real. Take the problem to God in prayer keep moving forward it is all about you. You matter your sanity is important. NDB's. Never change their

behaviors towards you hating behaviors worsen daily without warning. Leave and never look back. NDB's, will expose this behavior out of a devil's rage please pay attention do not entertain the monster within. The NDB, will demolish, destroy divine beings spiritually without warning in the presence of other NDB, who promote dysfunctional behaviors.

8. Narcissistic demonic beings harm without warning out of a wicked ignorance. NDB, like to play mental emotional mind games of deceit with mind, body, spirit and soul. Protect yourself physically, mentally and spiritually always know sincere angels are in the midst to assist and protect you. Divine assistance might not be visible but spiritually present at all times all you have to do is believe you have spiritual assistance spiritual assistance becomes a reality. You are never spiritually alone when in the midst of a narcissistic demonic beings with plans of behind the back deceit of misfortune. Narcissistic demonic beings are beneath you. They are the scum of the earth. NDB, despise hate divine beings in public and in secret.
9. Narcissistic demonic beings seek joy by watching divine beings suffer. This is an ultimate climax for NDB, thrive off of terror causing pain havoc in the lives of divine beings. Manmade hysteria. Manmade world pauses, virus, rules and regulations that are fitting only for a narcissistic demonic being plots of destruction. Separation of family. Deadly manmade virus created to kill, steal and destroy lives of divine beings. The shock of it all. Do not entertain narcissistic demonic behaviors once you know who and what you are dealing with immediately leave, vacate the premises. Do not entertain

wicked behaviors narcissistic demonic beings will hurt you by any means necessary emotionally, mentally, physically, spiritually, verbally. Narcissistic demonic beings do not give a damn about your spirituality or your well- being or your relationship with God. Remember, Narcissistic demonic beings enter the physical realm to kill, steal and destroy divine beings without a sincere righteous cause. Beware. The greatest lie ever told by narcissistic demonic beings is that God does not exist or hear your prayers. Pray to God the more prayer more power divine beings. NDB, tricky behaviors and lies are cruel by design narcissistic demonic beings never change their behaviors they rot with age become smelly stinky evil monsters who illegally house frail bodies for protection against the evil they feed the land. Spiritually this does not fool spirit.

10. Narcissistic demonic beings want to return back to the pits of a modern day, hell without punishment. NDB, expose insincere behaviors are severely punished spiritually for abusing divine beings without a sincere righteous cause its spiritual punishment it is only right spiritually fair remember nothing is hidden from the eyesight of God, especially the wicked behaviors of NDB, causing chaos, unnecessary drama, havoc among the lives of divine beings who do not bother anyone. May the mighty Gods of this bless universe dispose of all NDB, as divine beings travel through the blackhole
11. Narcissistic demonic beings are jealous and envy of your awesome, beautiful, talented spirit. Do not entertain narcissistic demonic beings for they are beneath you spiritually. NDB, are haters destroyers of divine beings, animal kingdom, fairies, earth angels, my autism is

beautiful angelic beings, space children, electrical beings, universal lovers, night birds, kings and queens of the universe who have a loving disposition a purpose in the universe. NDB, are soul killers, soul thieves, soul destroyers. NDB, want to be divine. NDB, want divine light, your glow, your spirituality, your God given design, genetics. NDB, are duplicators not spiritual originators, but imitators of a false reality who want to imitate light beings, divine beings. Narcissistic demonic beings are known for the curse of the evil eye narcissistic demonic beings hate beautiful spirits upon visual contact. NDB, can see your bright light blinding their dim light. Divine beings are unique by design. Divine beings are beautiful inside and out. Divine beings are spiritually blessed, highly favored in the eyesight of God. Divine beings are beautiful by design. Divine beings are leaders conquering NDB, motivators, inventors, spiritual being by design you are a super sexy natural being. You, are spiritually loved. You are a threat to any narcissistic demonic beings having a human experience. Narcissistic demonic beings are envious of your light, divine beings, God adores you. You are loved and protected by God and sincere angels

12. Narcissistic demonic beings display the scent of the ungodly an unclean being. Beware, some narcissistic demonic beings have a pungent foul body odor the teeth of the ungodly the breath of a dragon shit. Narcissistic demonic beings have a distorted view of the human experience of being physically spiritually clean for NDB, are filthy creatures. The hygiene process is non- existent for NDB. When narcissistic demonic beings speak, they exhale the scent of excrement on their mind out their mouth when speaking. Allegedly, Narcissistic demonic

beings are ancient monsters who over time design human costumes and mask worn to enter the physical realms to stop divine beings from achieving spiritual dreams and goals for the betterment of humanity. Narcissistic demonic beings enter the physical realm to kill, steal, and destroy light beings before divine beings complete their spiritual missions for the most-high God. Narcissistic demonic beings are ignorant the monsters believe they themselves are God. Silly monsters. The God above all Gods is watching every narcissistic demonic being in attendance. Spiritual school is in session unfortunately, NDB, time on planet E, has expired throughout the universe. Saturn Rising Enterprise has arrived for the grand exit the demise of all NDB, in attendance.

13. Narcissistic demonic beings don't dance they destroy, destroy divine beings with evil intent without a sincere righteous cause. NDB, believe they can control or stop actions of God by destroying divine beings with trickery of black magic used to destroy innocent divine beings set on the path of righteousness to restore love. Silly ignorant monsters, NDB, believed no one saw you commit crimes against the innocent and humble of the land
14. Narcissistic demonic being wicked spiritual bullies in the universe who pick on divine beings without a sincere righteous cause. Narcissistic demonic beings are useless in the eyesight of God, a disgrace of waste.
15. Narcissistic demonic beings enter from distant realms illegally uninvited for the adventures of a lifetime to destroy divine beings who enter planet earth for the betterment of humanity. Allegedly, NDB, are known for

having illegal human experience for the destruction of divine beings throughout ancient, current-day history. Narcissistic demonic beings cowardly hide behind costumes playing, pretending to be human. NDB, play emotional, mental, physical mind games with divine beings to destroy their minds. Narcissistic demonic beings wear a hidden mask to hide their true identity because they are cowards they strike in secret. The human eyes of divine beings have been conditioned, contaminated polluted to believe illusions of wicked narcissistic demonic beings who dwell on planet E, causing havoc for the humble of the land.

16. Narcissistic demonic beings are not aware history without the truth is a spiritual lie. Hidden truths will be spiritually exposed in due time. Narcissistic demonic beings blindly believe lies of narcissistic demonic beings who enter realms prior to the spiritual shift. The demise of NDB has arrived. History without the truth is a lie.
17. Narcissistic demonic beings lie, cheat and steal without a sincere righteous cause. Many beings visually witness or read about NDB, social dysfunctional behaviors daily but often ignore its exposure of evil for this is Allegedly, the norm of a social society under a wicked spell of NDB, control, conditioning minds of followers recruiting knew members to assist play a game of follow the narcissistic demonic belief rituals.
18. Narcissistic demonic beings do not change their behavior towards divine beings. Beware this is a false belief of an NDB, game to control you. Once evil always evil. There is no room for era in the eye sight of God. Message, NDB, dysfunctional cover is revealed. History without the truth is a lie. NDB, enter realms to kill, steal

and destroy without divine beings without a sincere righteous cause

19. Narcissistic demonic beings live in a false state of space and time believing wicked rules and regulations created by feeble minds are correct. The lifestyles of narcissistic demonic beings are ungodly. NDB, are eager to cause confusion, kill, steal and destroy divine beings for fame and fortune only to dwell in a false state of gratification of hell on planet earth.
20. Narcissistic demonic beings spread disease throughout the universe, emotionally, sexually, physically, and mentally. NDB, sole mission is to kill, steal and destroy divine beings. Narcissistic demonic beings are known to kill, steal and destroy by any means necessary be cautious during sexual gratification scan genital areas, always practice safe sex. You never really know who or what being you are entertaining spiritually or sexually due to narcissistic demonic beings entering through portals out of curiosity entertaining, inviting ancient evils of the blackhole to enter the physical realm without spiritual notification. Remember, divine beings are not the only being's species in the universe due to destructive acts of NDB, opening portals, dimensions inviting beings of other galaxies eagerly waiting to enter entertain, sample divine beings sexually, mentally, physically. Divine beings are sexy by design every being wants to sit in the midst of divine beings, have sexual adventures with divine beings. Many beings from other galaxies, planets, dimensions pass through planet earth every micro second of a second in the blink of an eye traveling through the blackhole in hopes of spiritual connections. Repeat. Please. Beware, be cautious in your

dealings because you never know in this day and time who or what being you are entertaining in this lifetime. Be cautious. Be aware of the invisible, hidden, narcissistic demonic beings in the universe who wears the mask of many faces because monsters are among us so are shapeshifters who live in costumes pretending to be human.

21. Allegedly, beings of metagalaxy enjoy forbidden sexual acts of sensual gratification. Remember your first orgasm the intense act feelings of what a human body can do is amazing electric stimulating experience for any being experiencing human sexual act. Sex is awesome divine beings should not have to die for orgasms or being sexy by design. Remember the most sexually beings of the metagalaxy are divine beings. Sex is a fabulous stress reliver stimulators of the ultimate orgasm are uplifting for the soul. Falling prey to intense feelings of seductive slow roaming finger tips of seduction all over your body is natural, just be cautious in your dealings. Planet earth is traveling through the blackhole you never no who or what being you will encounter meet or entertain while living, traveling through the blackhole. Passionate hot moist kisses mesmerize senses causing moist secretion of inviting liquid lava to cloud or invade sensual senses on a first date. Unknown narcissistic demonic beings seeking pleasures and seduction of participating bodies in motion enter physical realms ready to lay pipe or get laid by big pipe dream executives of satisfaction within seconds of meeting. Visiting beings of un-known star-systems are eagerly seeking divine beings, narc survivors, super freaks, bodies of heat, body with yummy tasty surprises hidden treats of satisfaction,

bodies of heat connecting coming together in union with feature pleasures of seduction of slow grinds of slip and slide. Thrill of fully dressed bumping, grinding, humping, rubbing, sampling erotic stimulating body spots of secret passion points engulfed electrical bolts of passion waves of deep seduction. Uninvited beings, erotic parties of magical pulsating rhythm of passion erupt inside bumping grinding tingling vibrating slow erotic dances of passion orgasms fill the air the thrill of sexual acts of nonstop licking, sucking, rubbing, bumping, touching fondling sensitive body parts once believed to be nonexistent suddenly become alive with excitement discovering hidden pleasure points connecting joining together for the ultimate orgasm of intense hot steamy sexual act for the fun of it all, 120,000,0000 positions of sexual gratification of beings traveling through the blackhole seeking willing participants to participate in a game of hide go get it galaxy sex. If divine beings decide to play sexual tag test the spirits, play with caution protect yourself at all cost you have been spiritually warned. Be cautious of the charming handsome large memorizing universal talking Penus. Male beings of hidden star-system called Stroke Island. Smile don't fall for the banana in the banana split or the golden clits of beings from galaxy Clitacoochie. Beware of ultimate clit, penal suckers these beings will literally eat, suck the life out of divine being. Divine beings are good and plenty the bomb-bay. Divine beings are the sexual candy bars that raises and uplifts the dead of boring head received from lower-level beings. Protect divine good love for deserving divine beings stop screwing narcissistic demonic beings.

22. Narcissistic demonic beings falsely wear costumes, cosmetic mask pretending to be human, NDB, monster is secretly plotting downfalls, causing chaos confusion and secret destruction by their ignorant dysfunction towards divine beings. Divine beings are here to slay NDB. Narcissistic demonic beings play the role of fake family, relatives, coworkers, associates, government officials, officers of the law, doctors, lawyers etc. Demonic behaviors I have experience or notice over the years of observation of NDB, I personally entertained, witness during my observation of narcissistic demonic beings I was entertaining without being aware of the presence of demons. I experience evil on sight prior to meeting greeting beings. The stare of evil eye upon contact, unfaithful in love, disloyal, betrayal by family those I trusted the most hated me, reward me evil for my good deeds towards them. Due to my physical family experience of hate towards me. I have no intentions of sitting in their presence. Never sit where you are not sincerely invited. Love, loves you narcissistic demonic beings despise, hate, create stories of demise for your downfall demonic beings get a climax for your hurt and pain. God sees all nothing is hidden.
23. Based upon my experience dealing, living, interacting, working with narcissistic demonic beings taught me a huge lesson monsters exist monsters are real. Monsters live in costumes pretending to be human. Archangels of the highest watch-towers stand guard observing the acts behaviors of narcissistic demonic beings posing as fake family members who target divine beings for destruction without a sincere righteous cause. Narcissistic demonic family members display acts and behaviors of evil, wicked, disrespect. These beings are

unaware of emotional intelligence they talk, criticize, judge talk about you behind your back wickedly smile in your face does black magic against you without knowing how abundantly blessed you are in the eyesight of the most-high God in the metagalaxy. NDB, posing as family members are determine to destroy divine beings at all cost know matter how spiritually sweet or kind the divine being maybe. This is the number one cause of mental illness in families throughout the universe. Narcissistic demonic beings are living among the living in costumes pretending to be our family members while purposely hating destroying family members. This form of spiritual abuse will drive any being insane during the human experience the damaging spiritual affects cause one to question God, love, the human experience. Remember. NDB's, enter planet earth to kill the essence of hopes, dreams and prayers of earth angels and divine beings for the betterment of humanity. NDB, sole mission is to destroy love of divine beings, kill the zest of life during the human experience by stealing desires, dreams with deceit, emotional, mental, physical abuse betrayal of causing havoc in the lives of divine beings. NDB, seek destruction of divine beings who enter on behalf of God for the betterment of humanity and love. NDB, sincere fakeness of it all is sincerely trifling behavior. Nothing is hidden in the spirit world. Angels of the highest spiritual courts are observing rude attitudes obscene hidden behaviors of narcissistic demonic beings posing as family members. NDB, posing as parents are being exposed all over the metagalaxy for their dirty evil wicked deeds of divine beings. What a treat for earth angels, divine beings to witness the fall of wicked NDB, who enter planet E, to kill, steal and destroy divine beings without a sincere righteous cause in the eye-sight of the most-high God above every God ever planted in the universe on the world stage of life. Welcome to God's Theatre. Where nothing is hidden in the eye-sight of the most-high God above every God ever planted in the universe.

Modern day ratchet narcissistic demonic behaviors against divine beings that are often unnoticed or unexpected

1. Narcissistic demonic being, gutter rat behaviors: will set up divine beings for any form of spiritual trauma, betrayal, deceit, rape, death, etc. Narcissistic demonic beings will smile in your face while deceiving you and playing mental games of fuckery trickery for their personal satisfaction of evil against you without a sincere righteous cause.
2. Narcissistic demonic beings stare of envy , jealousy behind your back: The evil eye: eye of deception trickery deceitful glares stares, questionable looks by narcissistic demonic being within the family, friends, coworker associates, who are born ugly in appearance.
3. Narcissistic demonic being black magic behavior: the casting of spells against divine beings, or their children for failure misfortune while smiling in face of the divine being while baking killer bread and cookies to die for your consumption this is for their own personal satisfaction.
4. Narcissistic demonic beings Jinkey spirit behavior: liar, thief, bad blood line, rotten disposition, seeks attention by being wickedly dishonest, deceptive in behavior. Lies about divine beings receives attention

of evil responses for pleasure attempts to distort image of divine being character with made-up created lies for demonic gratification

5. Narcissistic demonic beings hindering spirit behavior: dream killer, stalker, false associate, family, friend, the narcissistic demonic being that just won't leave you alone after the break-up, misfortune, cheater, lies, sexually transmitted disease, disloyalty, scandals experienced together. All, narcissistic demonic beings thrive on the energy of divine beings the NDB, lover that drives you mentally insane, you imagine 20 billion ways to kill the NDB, lover for poisoning your soul with insincere acts of false acts in love.
6. Narcissistic Demonic beings as parents: Parental behavioral patterns most experienced by divine beings: NDB, as parents physically, mentally, and verbally abuse, neglect their children out of ignorance. Hurt, harm, damages the child natural development. Narcissistic demonic beings only know how to be monsters not parents. Narcissistic demonic beings who wear the costume of a false self of parent causes severe damage to a divine being before the soul of the divine being is developed to handle the hidden spiritual reality my parents are real life monsters having an illegal human experiences. Divine beings who are experiencing any of these behaviors from your parents or parent Immediately seek help. Never sit, sleep, or stay where your spirit is not welcome. Leave immediately. Never look back never go back narcissistic demonic beings do not change monsters become worst with age do not trust narcissistic demonic beings once you realize who and what you

are entertaining. Never stay in an environment that is not respectful of your loving spirit. Sincere loving parents love and adore, appreciate their children's human experience. Narcissistic demonic beings as parents destroy divine beings human experience during early childhood development. Narcissistic demonic beings posing as parents talk down to their children judge and criticize the children for being who and what God created. Narcissistic demonic beings posing as parents cause destruction of ignorance in the lives of their children. Narcissistic demonic beings posing as parents fuck their kids up mentally unfortunately, this is the real cause of severe mental abuse and illness in the physical realm. Narcissistic demonic parents are cruel to their children, they have no respect or remorse for the safety of children. The universe is infested with monsters posing as parents. Help! Save the children

7. Narcissistic demonic parents enter the physical realm to kill, steal and destroy the righteous of the land. NDB's, posing as parents target divine beings, earth angels, space children, universal lovers, night birds, my autism is beautiful babies, fur babies, Ts-baby metagalaxy beauty dolls. Spirit recognizes spirit. I love you and your bold flamboyant style. Thank you for being apart of my human experience. In loving memory of Sylvester, never forgotten always remember with blessings of love. Do you want to funk with me? I put that on Mary had a little Doberman pitcher name Killah. She lived in Watts California among dragon, snakes and gutter rats. She was bold. She was everything. She was a Watts warrior. Narcissistic demonic beings target the innocent of the

land without a sincere righteous cause. Narcissistic demonic beings as parents destroy what they do not understand nor comprehend there are no mistakes, labels in the spirit world all souls are genderless. Remember we are traveling through the blackhole metagalaxy of new adventures new people, places and unique wonders of the universe no one knows who or what they will become upon their individual life experiences. Welcome to the metagalaxy of the black hole. Live life with caution be aware of the things that you can not see but are seen in the spirit world. Prayer is valid during the metagalaxy blackhole adventure during the human experience. Cover yourself in prayer for divine beings are being secretly watched by unknown beings from metagalaxies that are spiritually three feet away from a home or neighborhood you

8. Narcissistic demonic behaviors of Injustice against divine beings humble of the land: History without the truth is a lie. False allegations beliefs about certain beings out dated laws rules and regulations of narcissistic demonic beings in positions of power. Manmade chaos created for destruction of humanity. Thieves of ancient queens of hate, ignorance against women. Beware. NDB, kingdoms are falling the truth of divine women creators of life demand universal respect. Ancient mothers of humanity are causing kingdoms of NDB, to fall. The curse of the great divine is upon narcissistic demonic beings who go against divine beings. NDB, who play with fire will surely burn in hell for every ill illusion set against women who bring forth life. History without the truth is a lie.

9. Narcissistic demonic beings, behavior of love: Allegedly, NDB's are Incapable of love, emotional intelligence: Clueless to what is love. No real desire to experience true sincere love nor comprehend the essence or simple meaning of emotional intelligence. NDB's, thrive on social sex multiple sexual partners without proper hygiene or protection. NDB's, are horny little devilish monsters seeking more lovers to destroy the joy of sex. Allegedly, this is the norm in the City of Lost Angels. NDB's, wear a variety of mask be aware of their presence within the atmosphere for they are tricky dickie, Pluto pussy cunning in personality.
10. Narcissistic demonic beings wear the mask of many faces, beware, your emotional, physical sanity is at severe risk. Do not entertain narcissistic beings once you realize who and what you are entertaining flee the scene immediately without an explanation never look back. Never go back. Sincerity is sincere there is no room for era in this lifetime. Narc survivor, divine beings you are spiritually design, created, gifted to endure hidden wicked acts, behaviors of narcissistic demonic beings seeking your spiritual demise. Narcissistic demonic beings deliberately destroy divine beings. Ancient angels examine scenes of deceitful wicked behaviors and experiences the narcissistic demonic being caused during its reigns of destruction to destroy divine beings. Narc survivor explore happiness, happiness is seeking your awesome magnificent presence do not allow the shocking realization you entertain or sat in the company of narcissistic demonic beings or monsters unaware of their true identity. Monsters exist monsters are among the land living in costumes

pretending to be human. Divine beings who wear the mask or take on the role of a narc survivor sit in the company of archangels, spiritual guards of protection without being aware of who they are entertaining. Divine being enjoy, live your human experience wisely without fear of the short-term presence of narcissistic demonic beings. The day of narcissistic demonic beings has come to an end their reign is over. Divine beings are the righteous of the universe. God is real no matter what you hear, no matter what a situation looks like visually, when you sit in the midst of narcissistic demonic beings watch your back watch your surroundings beware of illusions, mental games of confusion. Allegedly, the veil of narcissistic demonic beings having illegal human experiences has been exposed, revealed in the physical realm by divine beings who destroyed narcissistic demonic beings in the past. On behalf of Queen, Chief Sabu of Saturn Rising Enterprise. In the name of truth of a blessed loving universe. No narcissistic demonic being, evil, toxic thought, word or weapon formed against, insert your name on the line: "_______________ shall not prosper against me any narcissistic demonic being who enter my path shall be cut off in the name of the most-high God above all the Gods in the universe. As a divine being by design. I am blessed to enjoy my human experience how I choose. I am successful, I am the righteous of the land a divine being. I boldly walk with spiritual giants in a blessed universe. Beware, my ancient ancestor angels of the highest spiritual courts take charge over my wellbeing during my human experience.

Dearest, God above all Gods of a bless universe bless all narc survivors. Our journey has been rough no one prepared us for interacting with narcissistic demonic beings posing as parents as the first teachers of our life in the physical realm. Many divine beings are still in shock of the experiences, entertaining, or living with a narcissistic demonic being posing as parents who destroy, demise, dismiss their children as if they do not matter. The load is heavy the pain of every scene hurts the truth of the matter is it is shocking when you realize you have been living among narcissistic demonic beings who purposely entertain other demons for the sake of your demise. Divine beings, matter. Divine beings are God's favorite. I am forever grateful for my spiritual journey of conquering NDB, set in my path to destroy me without a sincere righteous cause. Entertaining sincere angels of honor who assist me upon my earthly adventures of planet E. Undercover Saturn being by design, 5′4, supple honey caramel brown sugar skin proud ancient five thousand four hundred years in flight looking fabulously delicious. What can I say? Darling. I am of the righteous of Saturn Rising. My original design sugar hot spice all that is lovely, rare delightful energy of nice, spiritual by design. My journey is not hidden from the most-high Gods of the heavens. I have sat in the midst of NDB, having illegal human experiences. I had sexual encounters with NDB, who enter planet E, to kill, steal and destroy divine beings the righteous of the land. I can confirm my personal experiences dealing with narcissistic demonic beings posing as family, friends, lovers and associates set in my path to kill me mentally, spiritually took me by surprise. Attempt to steal my dreams ideas and style. I question God I was angry with God for allowing such an experience. My prayer request for divine beings who receive this spiritual message warning about narcissistic demonic beings living on planet earth be cautious in your dealings beware monsters are real. narcissistic demonic beings are demonic beings who enter to kill, steal, destroy spiritual beliefs, gifts, confuse, destroy your spiritual relationships with God, bless archangels of power. Bless the minds of every narc survivor planted in the universe bless divine beings in spiritual abundance bless divine beings to spiritually know who they are spiritually. Bless divine beings to see with spiritual eyes, witness narcissistic demonic beings in their path of destruction to know the truth about demonic destruction. History without the truth is a lie. Bless all narc survivors, divine beings who believe in your strength mighty power to destroy, conquer defeat narcissistic demonic beings in existence forever. NDB, play games of damage control, distort truth discourage minds with illusions of body and soul of divine beings for destruction. The conditioning acceptance of behavior of NDB's on planet E, is insanely outrageous know narc survivor wants to live with or be housed with narcissistic demonic beings who deliberately attempt to destroy divine beings without a sincere righteous cause. My prayer is that the reign of narcissistic demonic beings is over. Most-high God. Show up show out on behalf of narc survivors we are leaning and depending on the most-high God to correct this matter asap narcissistic demonic beings are out of control and in severe need of going back to hell asap.

The Goddess of Love, From Saturn Rising Enterprise.

The Goddess of Love sexy, proud Saturnarian. The Goddess of Love dwells on moon Phoebe in the beautiful city of Disco. Disco is rated the highest vibrational city in the Saturn Rising region. The city of Disco thrives on the joy of living in heavenly bliss, welcoming environment, smiles of love, peace, laughter, celebrations of success, chandeliers, exotic juices, vegan appetizers, city apparel, glitter make up, faux furs, satin, lace, latex, rainbow-colored pets of affection, true love of life. Disco dancing workouts, Disco dance skate parties after six. Disco dancing lunch breaks. Daily disco, house, trance parties. The city of Disco where musical interludes of Disco legends are played nonstop on radio free Disco 33.55 SSSLB Saturn Sexy Sensual Love Beats. Strictly for sexy cats, kittens seeking love. Santurnarian, elite divine beings of love shine brightly throughout metagalaxies distributing love to beings who have never experience love. The best of Donna Summer. I feel love is playing on the air waves in the city of Disco. What is a narc survivor? Can you eat it?

Darling,

A Narc Survivor is an ancient Noble Angel Rescue Champion. Praises be to all narc survivors in attendance. Slay darlings. Narc Survivors enter planet E, from metagalaxies for the betterment of humanity. Narc survivors endure, suffer the pain, injustices of NDB, traps set in the path of destruction for divine beings. Narc survivors known divine being spiritual soul survivors on Saturn Rising Enterprise. Narc survivors be proud of your journey you are true spiritual royalty. Spiritual warrior by design to endure, fight against wicked behaviors of NDB, sent to destroy divine beings. Divine beings are super stars in the heavens. The Great Gods of heaven are proud of divine beings who conquer defeat narcissistic demonic beings set in paths of destruction. Narc survivors who went before you are proud of you. Spiritual by design narc survivor beautiful bold spirit who has fought against the evils of narcissistic demonic behaviors and won. Blessed and highly favored narc survivors aka divine beings among planet E, who have entered to slay NDB, on behalf of love for the betterment of humanity. Here is a list of narc survivors spiritual sub-groups who live in metagalaxies in costumes pretending to be human while enjoying the human experience on planet E. Spiritual introductions of divine beings, earth angels, electrical beings, universal lovers, ts-baby dolls, star children, my autism is beautiful angelic beings, angelic nonverbal beings, angelic animal kingdom angels, angelic fairy angels, night birds, nature babies, ancient kings & queens of the beginning of time have re-entered celebrate, dance, vogue with high honors. Dance darling. Love is back. Celebrate. Darlings. Slay. Be true. Be happy. Shape Shifters of love work your magic upon the land of Lost Angels. Spiritual watchers of the universe dance the dance of seduction the power of love has arrive. Celebrate, love is present. Dance celebrate the vibration of love. Love is back. I am in love with love. Prayer warriors celebrate the vibration of love. Dance celebrate love, love beings display love plant seeds of love in the hearts of beings who need love. I. The Goddess of Love have fought against ancient narcissistic demonic behaviors of emotional, mental and physical abuse and won spiritually. I salute every narc survivor with sincere blessings for being a part of the movement of love for the betterment of humanity. May the abundance of love reign, rain down upon narc survivors. High honors blessings of love be upon all narc survivors for defeating narcissistic demonic beings. I, The Goddess of

Love is forever grateful the strength of mighty warriors, narc survivors who never gave up the spiritual fight no matter how hard the fight. Narc Survivors who fought with the power of prayer, guns in pockets of lace garter belts for protection, equality, simple peace, abundance of love. It's spiritual. Muah! I love you. I love you all. Sincere Blessings

Beware, NDB's. Saturn Rising Enterprise has arrived, prepared for battle. Swoop. Bang, Bang, Toot, Toot, Beep, Beep, Tweet. Tweet. Bang, Bang, Bang. This is a Saturn Rising Enterprise service announcement for all NDB, in attendance on planet E. Based upon request of Saturnarians, who secretly dwell on planet E, the commander of spiritual confidential affairs the agent's names, origins and planets are confidential. However, enclosed is a list of undercover narc survivor agents of spiritual federations who have destroyed NDB, throughout galaxies. Spiritual invisible spies are among planet E. Sincerely, Commander, Chief of operations, City Cat Lion Goddess Counsel of Loyalty and Love. Saturn Rising Enterprise. Universal Chronicles

Saturn Rising Enterprise. Universal Chronicles. City of Disco, undercover elite narc survivors, secrets partially exposed. Elite spiritual spies, detectives of the universe who dwell on planet E. Living in costumes pretending to be human while observing, behaviors of NDB, during the human experience of divine beings visiting constellations, galaxies, planets, known unknown star-systems unknown to man.

Love Goddess confidential universal files of spiritual being's human behaviors from metagalaxies throughout the universe. Divine being's aka narc survivors are spiritual royalty divine beings who live among planet E, in costumes pretending to be human their age span of 205 years and beyond. Noble Angel Rescue Champions. Narc Survivors Federal history of undercover agents are over five million years old spiritually working effortlessly for the betterment of humanity.

Spiritual Undercover Metagalaxy Elite Narc Survivors Federations:

Noble Archangel Rescue Consciousness Committee
Survivors B.C. Status: Valid movement

Nature Angel Reserve Conservatory Survivors A.D.
Status: Activated universal movement

Naïve Angel Rescue Committee Survivors A.D.
Status: Movement in motion

New Archangel Recruit Counsel Survivors A.D.
Status: Movement in motion

Nationwide Angel Redeemer Counsel Survivors B.C.
Status: Activated universal movement

Negiiza Ancestor Rescue Counselors Survivors B.C.
Status: Universal movement

Nimbus Angel Rescue Counselors Survivors B.C.
Status: Movement in motion

Nigel Angel Recruit Counsel Survivors. B.C.
Status: Universal movement

Native Angel Reality Counsel Survivors B.C.
Status: Universal movement

National Archangel Rescue Connoisseurs Survivors A.D.
Status: Movement in motion

New Angel Recommit Counsel Survivors A.D.
Status: Active universal movement

National Angel Recovery Counsel Survivors B.C.
Status: Active universal movement

Natural Angel Reactor Committee Survivors B.C.
Status: Active movement in motion

Necessary Archangel Rescue Counsel Survivors B.C.
Status: Active Movement in motion

Negrillo Archangel Recovery Counselor Survivors B.C.
Status: Active movement in motion

Neighborly Angel Rescue Counsel Survivors A.D.
Status: Active movement in motion

Noble Archangel Rescue Connoisseurs Survivors B.C.
Status: Active movement in motion

Network Angel Recovery Counselors Survivors A.D.
Status: Active movement in motion

New York Angel Recovery Counsel Survivors B.C.
Status: Activated movement in motion

New Angel Reality Counsel Survivors A.D.
Status: Active movement in motion

Disco 33.55 triple SSSLB4 Saturn Sexy, Sensual Love Beats

Disc Jockey Goddess of Love Soulivia Storm featuring Her Sidepiece Silk Sofine.

Goddess of Love, Soulivia Storm

Greetings, Welcome, Saturnarians. I am the mistress of ceremony. Soulivia Storm. Welcome to Saturn Rising radio free. Disco 33.55 triple SSSLB4 Saturn Sexy, Sensual Love Beats. Where love is sincere and true. Where Saturnarians, rely on God at all times know matter how a situation introduces or presents itself. Saturn Rising Enterprise introduces Saturn Sensual, Sexy, Jazz Concerts by the Sea of

Love. Two moons east of Saturn Springs. Black fish and Sea Monkeys rising by popular demand in the deep sea of love, will be hosting their annual meet and great all you can eat veggie buffet on moon Dion. This is for the rich and famous Saturnaires, from the producers of the sitcom the juicy lifestyle of Saturnarians, Beings of love are seeking companions eager to experience love. Congratulations, to Starzsah & Soogie Sights, on their fifth, year anniversary celebration of love. Love is beautiful knew love is sincere patient passions of love slow moving intense arousal of erotic sensual love. Love is forehead kisses before breakfast. Love is bathtub back scrubs erotic conversations wine and roses. Love is kisses of delightful surprising kisses of love, lust, passion of connecting on a spiritual level. Love is realizing it is impossible to stop love of divine beings from existing, it is just impossible. Long live love! It is a blessed sensuous sunny day on Saturn Rising. Love arrived love is seeking love. Love is in the air. Ooh. Lala. Swoop. Soo. Lala. Love. Love arrives dancing prancing in a beautiful international silver studded diamond sequin gown draped over galaxies, dimensions planets without diamond lace trimmed sequin pantie bottoms nor lace garter belt. Love is free to dance, express, live, love without titles of manmade label tags for identity purposes. Love is energy traveling throughout galaxies of present time pleasing emotions of divine beings living in costumes pretending to be human. Love just wants to dance, express love, live in love, love in love, enjoy love. This is Disco 33.55 triple SSSLB4 Saturn's Sexy, Sensual Love Beats. Love wants to dance. I feel love, I am in love with love

Good loving, good living, Saturnarians, Swoop. My fellow divine beings of love aka narc survivors. Good loving peace, blessings to you. Sincere, Good Loving. Soulivia Storm. It is impossible to ignore love when it is starring you in the face. Divine beings be bold in love, communicate express your love to the divine being who has a special place in your heart express how special they are to you. Do it today right now don't wait another minute it is impossible to ignore love when you are in love. This is Silk Sofine. Send bouquet flowers of love to the divine being you love. You are listening to Disco 33.55, Where love is alive in the atmosphere of love. This is Disco 33.55 Triple SSSLB4 Saturn's Sexy, Sensual, Love Beats. I am your sidepiece love doctor Silk Sofine, the great divine. I let my love shine. It is no secret that I am in love with Soulivia Storm the lady with the golden smile, my wife of 30 beautiful loving years. It's impossible to deny our love. Soulivia, Baby, please forgive me but some of the listeners need to know why I am so in love with you. Why did I create Wine and Roses Wednesdays for lovers only in your honor? The audience is curious about our love life. It is impossible not to love this woman. Soulivia, is the love of my life. The love I receive from Soulivia Storm, is surprise erotic house dates, freaky Fridays, play dates, stimulating erotic passionate games of you show me your intimate hot spots and I will show you my secret hot spots. Stimulating games of role playing in full costume. One of my favorites is Little Red Riding Hood. I play a damn good responsible humble handsome, sexy wolf its, the shape shifter in me. Love is shared bubble baths extra bubbles after work greetings of wine, fruit, head and facials.

Silk Sofine

I pay homage to my queen, I love her. I create my exotic mood with sexy music, fruit and veggie appetizers wine flutes. My love enjoys stimulating conversations of life that tend to become erotic in midsentence with intense body heat waves of seduction that take over the conversation, Sh. Listen to love hugs and kisses are present. Our love is sexual attraction sexual healing rhythms of love in love with love knowing nothing can break our bond the core of our love is sincere love of two narc survivors discovering true love enjoying love together, two beings becoming one being. I am in love with love. I love this divine Goddess of Love. My wife of thirty years the forever sexy, Mrs. Soulivia Storm. I love you, Baby girl.

Goddess of Love Soulivia Storm

Greetings. My king. I love you. Good Loving, divine beings special by design. I can sincerely say, I am in love with a narc survivor. The day I met Silk, my life changed forever as I knew it. I had given up on ever experiencing true love fore I only knew false love, love of narcissistic demonic being who live in costumes pretending to be human, family, friends, lovers. Narcissistic demonic beings never loved me but seek to secretly destroy the essence of pure love within me spiritually by unforbidden acts of betrayal, deceit and destruction. NDB, are incapable unaware of emotional intelligence of love based upon my experiences of love and my perception of love. I was emotionally, mentally, physically abused, broken, confused by my human experience without ever experiencing true love. It is impossible not to love Silk, a divine being by design, my personal angel in disguise. I am in love with a narc survivor.

I love you, Silk Sofine. You blow my mind with memories of compassionate love that is passionately divine. It's impossible to deny you deny your love for me. I sincerely love you. Silk Sofine. I love how you love me. I know that you love me you appreciate me you love me. Thirty years with Silk loving me unconditionally educating me spiritually about love and loving Silk more and more is what introduce me to love. It is impossible not to love Silk Sofine. Audience, this is Soulivia Storm, and, I am in love with an narc survivor and his name is Silk Sofine. All divine beings this is an open invitation, join us for our annual be bold in love, confess your love Saturday and Sunday Soul love connection buffet and picnic celebrating love, a day of wine and roses on moon Phoebe. Where lovers unite and love is present, sincere excited, thrilled to be appreciated and loved with a feeling among lovers of the metagalaxy. This is Soulivia Storm, Saying. Celebrate love, enjoy love. Surprise someone with a love letter. Love wants to entertain love start loving. Now it's time for our social report

Sunny Love'Rainz

Greetings & Swoop, local Saturnarians. I am Sunny Love'Rainz. Love is in air as we travel through the black-hole dress to impress, you never know who or what you might met while traveling throughout distant constellations, dimensions, galaxies, planets known-unknown star systems. Be cautious in your dealings be mindful other divine beings share the metagalaxy with you. On the flip side of the moon, divine beings, shape shifters by popular demand are vacationing on planet earth. Invisible beings who wear a variety of costumes and mask are vacationing in exciting galaxies, dimensions. Narcissistic demonic beings are traveling planets in-search of illegal affairs for beings willing to participate in feast of pleasure. The fabulous ancient invisible beings who pop in and out of the physical realm without notice of being caught or seen by the human eye have arrived for fun in costumes and mask for the human experience? Welcome to the life of divine beings who travel through the blackhole of surprise beings, places and things daily excitement. Allegedly, many beings of earth have entertained, dated, their guardian angels, angels, celestial beings without noticing their true identity due to the beauty of the mask or costume worn for the human experience. The beings of earth are visually stimulated beings if a being choose to wear a beautiful handsome costume or mask chances are that being will be successful in receiving welcoming sex from a being who greets beings with sexual healing upon entering earth

The soul of a being is colorless. You see there is no prejudice in love, love cannot and will not be stopped by narcissistic demonic beings who are clueless about love. Ha. Ha. Ha. Pardon my laughter narcissistic demonic being believe themselves to be destroyers of God, love, divine beings. Historical spiritual truths are being exposed daily. Love arrived all narcissistic demonic beings have been defeated and should immediately return back to the pits of hell they have escaped. Narcissistic demonic beings are in for a spiritual treat of truth from the heavens, money can't buy blessings in the upper room. Heaven is priceless. History without the truth is a lie. The truth of love can no longer be hidden the secret to living a successful life in the metagalaxy is love sincere love. Narc survivors welcome sincere love, love is here to stay this is the day of celebrating love. Celebrate love with a day of wine and roses or seductive games of passion with love of two divine beings becoming one unit by connecting spiritually. Stimulating erotic intense conversations about love are sexy ways to communicate love. Adult games of passion are fun, some of my favorites are suck, lick and blow or bump and grind slow dancing are sexy situations to consider or indulge games of sensual stimulation that arouses senses are the most fun. Keep love simple for the simple lovers I recommend. Backyard late night disco dancing, bump and grind during a full moon. Stimulating conversations tequila chips and salsa, peanuts. Exotic nachos. Slow intense sensual dance moves. Slow twerk your way into the bathroom share a bath or shower let love take over. Relax. This information is for lovers only. Welcome Love. This is Sunny Love'Rainz of Saturn sending out love. Today is Saturn Saturday Skate weekend event featuring me and my famous Saturn Sloppy Joe vegan burgers. Let's get sloppy. Sloppy Joes are always free at my station. Up next is, my beautiful wife T.T. Mrs. Tornado Thunder from Venus.

Saturn Saturday Skating Social Festival

Saturn Rising Enterprise Universal Chronicles Musical Interludes for Saturnarians in love.

Acid Jazz Saturn Rising Funk: A minor featuring City Cat & The Night Birds from Birdland

Welcome, Divine beings, aka Narc survivors, Saturnarians, Of love. Welcome Saturnarians, who are in love with love. Saturnarians, experiencing love for the first time, love is in the air. Please enjoy the entertainment

I'm in Love with a Narc survivor

Night Birds

I'm in love. I'm in love. I'm in love. I'm in love. I'm in love. I'm in love with a narc survivor

I'm in love. I'm in love. I'm in love. I'm in love. I'm in love. I'm in love with a narc survivor

City Cat

I'm in love with a narc survivor. One two three four five six seven the love of a narc survivor must be from heaven. Sweet dreams come true I'm in love with a narc survivor its true this vibration of love keeps me high, soooo high. I'm in love with a narc survivor I'm in love with a Soul survivor that respects my situation I'm in love with a narc survivor. Oh, that magic feeling of love I'm in love with a narc survivor. I'm in love. I'm in love. I'm in love. I'm in love. I'm in love. I'm in love with a narc survivor

Night Birds

I'm in love. I'm in love. I'm in love. I'm in love. I'm in love, I'm in love with a narc survivor one two three four five six seven the love of a narc survivor must be from heaven. I'm in love. I'm in love. I'm in love. I'm in love. I'm in love. I'm in love with a narc survivor One two three four five six seven the love of a narc survivor must be from heaven. I'm in love. I'm in love. I'm in love. I'm in love with a narc survivor

City Cat

Oh, that magic feeling of love. I'm in love. I'm in love I'm in love. I'm in love. I'm in love. I'm in love with a narc survivor, this love is wiser. I'm in love. I'm in love. I'm in love. I'm in love. I'm in love. I'm in love. I'm in love with a narc survivor. I'm in love. I'm in love. I'm in love. I'm in love. I'm in love with a narc survivor. I'm in love with a narc survivor. I'm in love with a narc survivor. I'm in love. I'm in love

~ Commercial Trailer

Turn the minizine upside down for another adventure

Greetings. it is time for a Saturn Rising Enterprise episode of Trilogy of Narc Survivors

Sylvania Georgia State Asylum

Severe winter storm flashfloods surprise the residents with heavy winds huge dark gray clouds bursting with golf ball size hail falling from the skies. The humongous full moon displays the moods feelings of divine beings from other galaxies, dimensions and planets by a magnetic field of intergalactic forces of the universe. Enclosed are undercover files of the ancient divine beings from different galaxies, dimensions and planets in the universe who seek the assistance of Dr. Sah'zael.

Patient: Undercover Ancient Goddess 8th Dynasty

Black Cat Federation city of Thebes; Narc survivor 888

Dr. Sahza'el, Patient states, dated February 2, 2020 Patient unfair work environment, work-related trauma, mistreated, under paid for angelic services by the Lost Angels Unidentified School District, twenty years of service. No. Thank you plaque for twenty years of service. No bonus payments or dinner coupon for a complimentary meal nor a tarjae', twenty- dollar gift card. No party of service, gift from the administrative staff, the principal or a thank you note of service. Letters of appreciation from staff & students that I assisted. Special education assistant: The assignment, chosen mask worn throughout planet E. undercover mission of sincerity among divine beings employed, working side by side with narcissistic demonic beings. NDB's, who are being secretly monitored by the most-high Gods of spiritual commanders, judges, lawyers of the highest courts of heaven for their insincere behavior toward divine beings without being aware of the divine's true spiritual identity or purpose within the educational setting. Nothing is hidden in the eyesight of the most-high mother, father God, all is visible

Patient states, "NDB's, posing as educators sent to kill, steal and destroy divine beings upon arrival of the educational experience are going to hell for their unfair behavior towards divine beings. NDB's, have sat in the company of elite divine beings only to disappoint the spiritual realm by their distasteful behavior against ancient divine beings in disguise posing as special ed assistants employed by the Lost Angels unidentified school district. Doctor, I was taunted by NDB's, posing as educators, administrative staff with horrible file dispositions of the true monsters that they are deep inside underneath their false mask worn daily while at work. Doctor, I dealt first hand with NDB, witches with funky dispositions who wore upside cross tattoo to work without shame and publicly to torment me daily at work. There was no help or assistance for me, I was a special ed asst being tormented daily by NDB's. Warlocks are hired many paid to pass the c-best. Snakes, trap tramps, gutter rats, hood rats, the office staff of monsters who live in the city of Lost Angels educating, destroying divine beings because NDB believe as an NDB, educator NDB, have that right. How dare you sit in the midst of innocent children, divine beings wearing humanoid costumes, pretending to be human while secretly, being vicious, vile, wicked educators, employers, employees who purposely use defamation of character against me when I entered to assist or provide a service in any educational setting. How dare you narcissistic demonic beings of the Lost Angels unidentified school district did not protect me from all hurt, harm and danger while being employed with a bunch of monsters, NDB's. I was hit in the face with a hard basketball at age five- duce. The NDB, worker comp doctor gave me one day off from work. Wow. Really. Sincerely beware of the NDB, posing as doctors of secret mental destruction.

Dr. Sahza'el. I appreciate you. You are sincere and true. You sincerely care about your patients you do not care about the money. Doctor, you sincerely care about your patients. What dimension, galaxy or planet are you from. You are not a Plutonarian. You are not an earth being. You are different. Where ever you are from, Dr. Sahzael, you have a lot of love in your heart. You are the righteous. Tell me are you an ancient divine being having a human experience? I'm curious enquiring minds would like to know.

Dr. Sahza'el

Ha. Ha. Ha. My dear, City Cat you are very unique yourself. I am flattered, intrigued by your beauty and curious nature, I admire my patient's courage strength. Many of my patients have experience hell on earth at the hand of NDB's posing as human beings such as yourself. I am here to help, heal and repair the heart and souls of the broken, on behalf of the most-high God out of sincere love for the betterment of humanity. I love helping my patients. I love to see my patients healed and happy.

High Priestess aka the infamous City Cat

MMM. Really now. Whatever. I still respect you. MMM. Back to my horrible NDB, experiences while I was an employee of The Lost Angels Unidentified School District. The workers comp doctor, sincerely did not have my best interest at heart. Me being spiritually intuitive could feel read the hidden verbal expression. I was nothing and my work-related trauma meant nothing to the NDB, posing as a medical doctor. I currently have headaches to this day from being hit in the face with a hard basketball with great force. How dare you, inconsiderate NDB, doctor. NDB, lack compassion, empathy for divine beings. I fell, down at work on location at an elementary school. I was escorting children to the bus and out of nowhere, I was pushed down with great invisible force. I damaged my ribs, knees, wrist and hand. The doctor did not offer me a walking cane, crutches outside of all that drama, the universe is contaminated with NDB's posing as health care officials. I have observed their ill behavior for fifty- four years in physical sense. Spiritually, I am five thousand four hundred years of age, the 5th dynasty of Thebes, (BCE) I am an ancient High-Priestess and I still look good in-spite of all the deceptive acts caused by NDB, gang stalking, black magic used to kill, steal and destroy me. The inconsiderate NDB, put in my path for destruction are in serious spiritual trouble no being disrespects ancient high-priestess. That is a severe spiritual crime I have no mercy or pity for the beings responsible for such cruel behaviors against me. NDB, Your, wicked acts, behavior are unforgettable save the insincere apology for the gate keeper of your private hell. The ancient High-Priestess of Saturn Rising arrived to expose NDB, in the educational system unfortunately, monsters are real and that is a known fact. I have lived, worked among filthy NDB, posing as educators of destruction. I innocently, entertained NDB, without being aware of the signs and fact that I was entertaining real-life monsters. My job is done here this information divine beings will be able to discern between the spirit if it is an NDB, with the breath of a dragon shit or if it is a divine being having a human experience. In closing lower-level beings of a life are infested with the energy of NDB, who enter the physical realm to kill, steal and destroy divine beings. Live cautiously acknowledge your ancestors in prayer. Know matter what any NDB, says. God is real nothing is ever hidden in the eye-sight of God. Angels are among the physical realm living in costumes pretending to be human for the betterment of humanity on behalf of love.

June 4.2021

Synopsis:

Saturn Rising Enterprise Universal Chronicles is a Saturn based science fiction, edgy spiritual tale, based upon the undercover lifestyles of divine beings from other dimensions, galaxies and planets who secretly enter or visit planet earth daily due to the opening of portals that were to remain close for spiritual reasons. Planet earth is traveling through the black-hole like a taxi working pick-ups & drop-offs in old New York, New York, for beings curious about the human experience, without being aware or spiritually informed of the spiritual situations at hand all of hell has broken loose. The spiritual rules and regulations have been broken, destroyed by narcissistic demonic beings who have escaped from the pits of hell. Narcissistic demonic beings have entered the physical realm illegally to kill, steal and destroy divine beings without a sincere righteous cause other than ignorance. Saturn Rising Enterprise Universal Chronicles takes the reader on a journey and the adventures of divine beings experiencing the human experience while living, vacationing or visiting planet earth. Divine beings are performing live just beneath the heavens. Welcome to Gods theatre. Where nothing is hidden in the eyesight of God and divine angels. This story is told by ancient divine beings also known as Saturnarians. Saturnarians who enter planet earth living in costumes pretending to be human while working spiritually undercover to destroy narcissistic demonic beings who enter the physical realm to kill, steal and destroy divine beings who enter the physical realm on behalf of the most-high mother-father God above every God ever planted in the universe for the betterment of humanity and the rebirth of love.

Author Bio:

My physical name T. L. Nthrly. Please respect my creative individuality, address me as Trillionaire High Priestess of the Sun, by way of Saturn Rising Enterprise. I entered this realm unique with the creativity to write. I am an ancient soul. I have written in many books, I have lived many lifetimes my life stories have been erased, hidden, destroyed out of hate, ignorance and rage due to my beauty only to keep my presence unknown. History without the truth is a lie. I exist and I still look good. I am ancient but ripe for picking, I am well preserved. I am five thousand four hundred years of age, 8th Dynasty of Thebes. I entered this realm on behalf of God and not that of man. I am a prayer warrior by design. I adore and acknowledge God, my awesome divine ancestors and angels. I believe in the faith of a mustard seed. I sincerely believe in the most-high mother- father, God who is above all Gods of the universe. I believe that the clouds are sincerely the dust of their feet. I know for a fact that nothing is hidden from the eyesight of God. Nothing is hidden from the spirit world. Welcome to God's theatre where nothing is hidden when it comes to the world stage of life featuring the reality that planet earth is infested with narcissistic demonic beings having illegal human experiences. True story. I was a high school drop-out. I, asked God for a high school diploma. I had small limited beliefs know one ever discuss the importance of a good education or education at all, the abusive effects of abandonment, neglect and mental taunting are the number one reason people have mental health issues. The effects of being raised by narcissistic demonic beings posing as parents or guardians having an illegal human experience as family causes severe spiritual trauma to a divine being mental state. To my surprise God was listening to my prayer request for a high school diploma. I graduated from Los Angeles Trade Technical College earned my Associate Art Degree in Liberal studies, certificate in journalism. I became the editor of the Trade Winds Newspaper. With a desire for higher knowledge, I earned my Bachelors of Science, received my Master's Degree in Human Behavior from National University. My confirmation, God is real hidden angels exist. The greatest lie ever told by NDB, is that God does not exist. The spirit of God is among the living. Welcome to God's Theatre. Where every act, behavior is seen nothing is hidden in the eyesight of God.

MAY 5. 2022 GOALS ACCOMPLISHED.

THANK YOU, MY BLESSED ANCIENT ANCESTORS OF THE HIGHEST SPIRITUAL COURTS, OF LOVE WHO PROTECT ME FROM THE INVISIBLE FORCES OF EVILS FROM WICKED BEINGS WHO WORK BEHIND YOUR BACK OR IN SECRET BECAUSE THEY ARE IGORNANT ANCIENT BEINGS WHO ARE MODERN DAY COWARDS.

www.ingramcontent.com/pod-product-compliance
Lightning Source LLC
LaVergne TN
LVHW010501160826
845677LV00012B/2599

* 9 7 9 8 8 4 6 5 7 7 9 0 9 *